With gentleness and hope, *Healing Feelings* helps children understand and cope with mental illness in the adults who are important to them. This is a wonderful resource for kids who are struggling with their parents' or other adults' pain.

—Jacqueline Golding, Ph.D.
psychologist, Pleasanton, CA, and professor,
University of California, San Francisco
Author of *Healing Stories: Picture Books for the Big
and Small Changes in a Child's Life*

The rhythm and rhyme have a lovely cadence that children will really enjoy. Leslie has captured the idea of emotional pain through a child's viewpoint, children and parents alike will relate to this lovely imagery.

—Mary Ruth Cross, M.S., M.F.T.
licensed marriage and family therapist, San Ramon, CA and California Association for Play Therapy (CALAPT) Executive Board, member-at-large and past president of CALAPT San Francisco Bay chapter.

ISBN: 978-1-947247-76-5
Healing Feelings
Copyright © 2010, 2017 by Leslie Baker, M.A., MFT. All rights reserved.

Yorkshire Publishing
3207 South Norwood Avenue
Tulsa, Oklahoma 74135
www.YorkshirePublishing.com
918.394.2665

Healing
FEELINGS

A healing story for children coping
with a grownup's mental illness

by Leslie Baker M.A.,MFT

YorkshirePublishing
www.yorkshirepublishing.com
Write Now.

Dedication

To Paul and Tori, whose love has sustained me, inspired me, and filled me with immeasurable joy.

Acknowledgements

Special thanks to my family, friends,
and colleagues for their gracious support
throughout this project.

What are feelings?
I want to know,
They're in our minds,
our hearts, our souls.

Feelings help share what's inside us,
And help our minds know
where to guide us.

Feelings come in all kinds and sizes,
They're like a family
that lives inside us.

There are feelings for almost anything;
Some help us cry; some help us sing.

Here are some feelings
that we know best;
Together, we can find the rest.

There's happy,

sad,

angry,

mad,

There's scared,

shy,

and even glad.

We may feel confused, tired, and giggly.
We may feel bored, quiet, or even wiggly.

Sometimes we feel excited and surprised.
Sometimes we feel strong
and filled with pride.

Of course there's weird, silly, and funny.

Sometimes we feel really goofy

or clumsy.

These feelings are just a very few;
There's more to say
before we're through.

You see, in most of us,
our feelings work just right.
They help us smile
and feel safe at night.

But sometimes feelings slip and slide
And are not a very helpful guide.

Sometimes feelings can get sick,
And put grownups in a fix.

Sometimes worry will not leave,
Which makes it hard to even breathe.

Sometimes sadness comes to stay,
Leaving grownups no time to play.

And then the worry comes once more,
They wish it would just
go out the door.

These mixed up feelings can feel so bad,
Making our families feel mad and sad.

We miss the way our grownups
laughed and played,
Now they feel yucky
and want to hide away.

But there is hope, dear little ones:
A "feeling healer" needs to come.

"Feeling healers" make it so
Our feelings will not feel so low.

Sometimes the healers talk to them,
And then feelings work all right again.

A doctor may help heal feelings too,
Helping the feelings not feel so blue.

This can straighten them out quick
So the feelings won't feel so sick.

Some talking, time, and love combined,
Can help the feelings feel just fine.

When those we love feel good again,
We can get back to being friends.

A truth to know before you go:
There is never anything you can
do or say,
To make a grown-up's feelings,
feel mixed up in any way.

Help from "feeling healers" can
help a grow-up's feelings
find a way to feel better with
each day.

Remember, even when their
feelings weren't feeling well,
They loved you all the time, even
if you couldn't tell.

Keep love in your heart and good
thoughts in your mind.
Together we can all help feelings
heal with some help & time.

CPSIA information can be obtained
at www.ICGtesting.com
Printed in the USA
LVHW070139160222
711262LV00009B/224